IN PATHS OF PERIL

J. MACDONALD OXLEY

Copyright © 2023 Culturea Editions
Text and cover : © public domain
Edition : Culturea (Hérault, 34)
Contact : infos@culturea.fr
Print in Germany by Books on Demand
Design and layout : Derek Murphy
Layout : Reedsy (https://reedsy.com/)
ISBN : 9791041819454
Légal deposit : July 2023

IN PATHS OF PERIL

CHAPTER I

FROM THE OLD WORLD TO THE NEW

The defence of the city of La Rochelle by the Huguenots, when for more than a year they defied the whole power of France under the leadership of Cardinal Richelieu, must ever remain one of the most heroic and soul-stirring chapters in history.

For the sake of their faith these noble people endured the pangs of hunger, the perils of battle, and the blight of pestilence, until at last, their fighting men being reduced to a mere handful, with broken hearts they were compelled to surrender. It was a terrible time for the weak and the young. Nearly one-half of the population of the city died during the siege, and those who survived formed a gaunt, haggard, miserable band, more like scarecrows than human beings.

Among them were a maiden of twenty and a boy of twelve years of age, whose fortunes we shall follow in these pages. She was Constance de Bernon, the only daughter of one of the most important families, and he, Raoul de Bernon, her nephew, now an orphan, both his parents having perished in the dreadful days of the siege.

Not all the horrors she had witnessed, nor the sufferings she had borne, in the least degree shook Constance's fidelity to her faith. She was of the stuff which makes martyrs, and would have died at the stake rather than renounce her religion. Right glad, therefore, was she when her parents succeeded in effecting their escape from old France, where only persecution awaited Protestants, and making their way across the Atlantic Ocean to the new France, where it was possible to be true to one's belief without having to suffer for it.

The de Bernons settled in what was then known as Acadia, now the Province of Nova Scotia, and began life again amid the wildness of the land which the Micmac and Melecite Indians had hitherto held as their hunting-ground. Raoul accompanied them. Since the loss of his parents his whole heart had gone out to Constance. Never was aunt more beloved by nephew. It might indeed with truth be said that he fairly worshipped her, and found in her companionship the chief solace for his great bereavement.

While to the older people the change from the comfort and security of their former life at La Rochelle to the crude and hard conditions of their new home could not help being a very trying one, Raoul, on the contrary, was rather pleased with it. There was no going to school, nor learning of lessons, except when his aunt could now and then spare an hour to spend with him over the few books they had been able to bring. He lived out-of-doors for the most part, and had no difficulty in finding plenty to occupy his time.

He was a sturdy lad, with a bright, strong countenance, which gave good promise for the future if only he kept in the right path; and he made many friends, not only among the settlers, but also among the Indians, some of whose camps were always near at hand.

"It seems to me you do not miss La Rochelle very much, Raoul," said Constance to him as they sat at the door of the house in the quiet of the evening, when all the work of the day was over. "You are quite happy here, are you not?"

The colour came into the boy's face at his aunt's words, for although she did not so mean it, her question seemed to imply that he was forgetting his former home and the dear ones he had lost.

"I do like it here," he replied, lifting his big brown eyes to hers. "It is very different from La Rochelle, I know, but——" and here he hesitated so long that Constance with a smile took up the sentence.

"But you'd rather live in the woods than in the city—that's it, isn't it, Raoul? I quite understand, and I don't blame you in the least. You're fond of adventure, and you're glad to be where there's apt to be plenty of it. How would you like to go with me to Cape Sable?"

"I'm ready to go with you anywhere, Aunt Constance!" was the prompt and hearty response. "But why are you going to Cape Sable?"

It was now Constance's turn to blush, and very charming she looked as she answered in a low tone with her face turned away:

"I am to be married soon, Raoul, to Monsieur La Tour, and he is going to take me to Cape Sable, where he has his fort."

Raoul sprang to his feet excitedly. The idea of his beloved aunt belonging to somebody else hurt him cruelly. It filled his heart with jealousy, and he exclaimed in a tone of passion:

"You're going to be married, Aunt Constance, and to leave us all! What is that for? Why couldn't you stay with us? We are so happy here."

Constance smiled with pleasure at the vigour of his speech, and putting her arm about his neck affectionately, said:

"You surely would not have me live and die an old maid, would you, Raoul? And Monsieur La Tour will make such a good husband for me!"

Raoul sighed as he warmly returned his aunt's caress. His protest was foolish, of course, and, after all, if she was going to take him with her to her new home, what would be the difference?

"Oh, yes, I suppose so," he answered. "But I didn't know. Please tell me all about it."

So Constance went into particulars, Raoul listening with profound interest.

Charles de la Tour, who was also a Huguenot, had now been for a number of years in Acadia, carrying on an extensive business in fishing and fur-trading, and had just built a strong fort at Cape Sable, which he called Fort St. Louis. Of this establishment he had invited Constance to become the mistress, and she had given her consent. Yet, although she loved de la Tour, who was a handsome, genial, daring man such as easily win a woman's heart, she did not want to part with her nephew, and de la Tour made no objection to his accompanying her, especially as he himself must needs be often absent from the fort on business expeditions for months at a time, and Raoul would then be good company for his wife.

So in due time it all came about as was arranged, and Raoul found himself settled at Fort St. Louis with his new uncle, whom he greatly admired and respected. This fort, placed at the extreme south-east point of what is now Nova Scotia, looked out over the restless waters of the Atlantic, and kept an eye upon the ships passing by to the Bay of Fundy or to the New England ports. It was very strongly built of stone, and mounted many cannon which Raoul longed to see in use. A snug harbour lay to the east, where de la Tour's vessels could anchor in safety from any storm, and inland stretched vast forests, which fairly swarmed with game, from the lively rabbit to the gigantic moose. What with fishing, trapping and hunting, rowing, sailing and swimming to his heart's content, Raoul was in no danger of finding the time hang heavy on his hands.

CHAPTER II

THE GREAT BEAR HUNT

There were many tribes of Indians scattered over Acadia—Abenakes, Etechemins, Micmacs, Openagos, and so forth, in whom Constance de la Tour took a very deep interest. She was full of zeal to teach them the Christian religion, and how to improve their way of living; and she went about from village to village, and from wigwam to wigwam, with wonderful patience striving to reach the hearts of the pagans, and help them to better things; so winning their love that she came to be esteemed as the guardian angel of their children.

Raoul usually accompanied her on these journeys, and strange enough were many of the places they visited. Now it would be a mere huddle of huts that looked like inverted wash-tubs, or again what seemed a cluster of large-sized hen-coops, or perhaps a big shed a hundred feet long with sleeping stalls below, and a loft above for the children, having neither windows nor chimney, and inclosed by a heavy oak stockade.

Whether big or little, these odd dwellings swarmed with squaws and children, and while his aunt was speaking to the elder folk, Raoul would always find amusement with the youngsters.

Many useful things did Madame de la Tour teach her dusky pupils— the way to bake bread, how to raise corn, pumpkins, and melons, the mode of preserving the fruit that was so plentiful in the autumn, and the art of making maple-sugar, all of which helped to benefit them, no less than the Gospel message she never failed to give also. She was the first missionary to these wild children of the forest in Acadia, and her memory is still enduring and fragrant because of the good she wrought amongst them. Raoul, vastly as he admired his aunt's devotion, could not of course be expected to share in it to any great extent, but since his idea of life was to have as good a time as possible—and he much preferred going on these expeditions to being cooped up in the fort—it suited him all right that she should be so zealous as she was.

Tramping through the vast green forests, or paddling in birch canoes over the clear water of smooth-running streams, there was always something new to be seen, and at any time an adventure might happen. In the autumn after their coming to Fort St. Louis, a great bear hunt was arranged to take place at the Tusket River, and Raoul was full of excitement about it. The plan was certainly as daring as it was novel, for the bears were not to be killed when found, but driven with clubs and switches towards the village, where arrows and spears and sharp appetites awaited them.

"I do hope there'll be plenty of bears," exclaimed Raoul to his aunt the evening before the hunt. "Won't it be exciting when they get them started, and they try to escape? I think I'll go out after the bears, and not wait at the village for them to come—that will be too tiresome."

"Whatever you do, Raoul, take good care of yourself," said Madame, patting him upon the shoulder. "You are my boy, you know, and I should be very sorry if anything were to happen to you."

Raoul smiled confidently as he drew himself up to his full height.

"Oh, there's no fear of me. I've had too much to do with bears to let any of them hurt me."

Madame smiled fondly back at him as she responded:

"You certainly look as if you ought to be able to take care of yourself. You are a fine big fellow, Raoul, and I pray God your life may be a long and happy and useful one."

The bear hunt was well organized under the direction of Madame, who had a genius for command. Raoul preferred going into the forest with the beaters to remaining at the village, and set off in high glee, the party being chiefly composed of the young men of the tribe.

It was the season of grapes, and the vines, which climbed in wild profusion to the very tree-tops, were laden with the luscious fruit which Bruin dearly loved. The hunters, therefore, were in no doubt as to where to seek their prey. Armed only with light clubs and supple switches, they dashed into the forest, darting this way and that, each one eager to be the first to find a victim. Raoul joined forces with an Indian lad of his own age named Outan, and it was understood that they were to stand by each other. Beside his club Raoul had a good hunting-knife in his belt, but he carried no fire-arms.

Pressing forward with reckless haste, they came to a place where the grape-vines fairly smothered the trees which supported them.

"Ah-ha!" exclaimed Outan exultantly. "Plenty bear here, for sure!" and the words had but left his lips when he gave a cry of joy and pointed excitedly to a tree, whose leaves were shaking, although there was not a breath of wind.

Raoul gazed in the direction indicated, and his heart gave a bound when he caught sight of a dark body that the leaves only half concealed.

"There he is! I see him!" he cried; "a great big fellow, and he's coming down!"

Running to the foot of the tree, the boys began to shout up to the bear, calling him names, and daring him to come down.

But, instead of obeying them, the big black fellow, one of the largest of his kind and in superb condition, turned about, and proceeded to climb higher.

"Hullo! that won't do," said Raoul in a tone of disappointment. "We'll never get him down that way. Let us throw stones up at him."

Accordingly they began to bombard the animal with stones, Raoul, who was a capital shot, succeeding in hitting him more than once. Yet this did not help matters at all. On the contrary the bear only climbed the higher. Then Outan proposed to climb an adjoining tree, taking some stones with him, and then to drive the creature down. Raoul thought the idea an excellent one, and took up his station at the foot of the tree with his club in readiness for immediate use. Outan went up the tree with the ease of a monkey, and gaining a good position above the bear shouted fiercely at him, while he threw the stones with accurate aim. Thus assailed from this unexpected quarter, the bear was panic-stricken, and started down the tree at utmost speed.

"Look out! bear's coming!" yelled Outan, and Raoul, with every nerve quivering, and his muscles as tense as bow-strings, grasped his club until his knuckles went white.

Tail foremost, the heavy animal shuffled down the tree-trunk with astonishing agility, and, reaching the ground on all fours, turned to face Raoul.

CHAPTER III

SETTING A BAD EXAMPLE

Up to this moment Raoul, carried away by the excitement of the hunt, had not stopped to consider what he should do if the bear happened to show fight instead of running away, but now he found himself face to face with the creature, which was evidently in no very good humour at having been so rudely disturbed while feasting on the grapes.

Growling fiercely the bear charged at Raoul, who darted off, shouting:

"Quick, Outan, quick! Come, help me!"

By dodging in and out among the trees he could keep out of the bear's clutches; but this complete change of programme was not at all what he had counted upon, and it was with great relief that presently he saw not only Outan, but several other Indians coming to his aid. Shouting and swinging their clubs they attracted the animal's attention from Raoul, who was fast losing his breath, and from being the pursuer the bear now became the pursued.

He was wise enough to see that the odds were against him, and made off at a shambling gallop which the hunters found it difficult to keep up with. Their object being to drive the bear towards the village they must needs keep him going in that direction, and this they found no easy task. It would almost seem as if he suspected their purpose, so hard did he try to go off at a tangent instead of straight ahead; and more than once Raoul well-nigh despaired of their succeeding in their object, and regretted that he had not brought his musket with him. But the Indians were not to be fooled. The bear was too fine a specimen to lose, and they spared neither their lungs nor their muscles as they kept up the pursuit with unflagging zeal. It certainly was a curious way of hunting bears, and if Bruin had only known how powerless his persecutors really were, he would, no doubt, have freed himself from them in short order. He was too badly frightened, however, to perceive the truth, and did his best to keep out of range of the menacing cudgels, while all the time the village drew nearer, where his fate awaited him.

Raoul would have liked very much to reach the village ahead of the bear, but although he ran his very best, he was left well in the rear, and when he came up the big black creature had already been dispatched.

"You poor fellow!" said Raoul as he passed his hand over the rich, glossy black fur, a qualm of pity succeeding the lust of the chase now that the excitement was over. "You did your best to get away from us, but we were too many for you. It was not just a fair fight, was it?"

Several other bears had been secured, and when the hunt was over, and the Indians had all gathered again, some strange ceremonies took place. Into the mouths of the slain bears smoke from an Indian pipe was blown by the hunters, and at the same time each lifeless creature was begged not to hold any hard feelings because of what they had suffered. Then the bears' heads, painted and decorated, were set on high, and the savages sang the praise of the Acadian king of beasts, after which the well-cooked bodies were divided amongst the hungry people, who feasted upon them greedily. Madame and Raoul had their share of bear-steak, and then the former took advantage of the quiet which followed the feast, to talk to these heathens about the Great Spirit whom she was so anxious they should learn to love. She was listened to with great attention by the Indians, because she had won their hearts, not only by her lovely character, but also by her many generous deeds and gifts.

But they were, for the most part, slow learners of the new and better way. The grizzled old chief, to whom Madame with infinite patience was teaching the Lord's Prayer, made a quaint objection.

"If I ask for nothing but bread," said he, "I shall have no more moose nor sweet cakes," referring to some toothsome cake that Madame had herself baked as a present for him.

After Madame had spoken, the young folks fell to sky-larking, while the elders smoked their pipes, and Outan, who was fond of teasing, raised a big laugh at Raoul's expense by telling how the bear had dropped from the tree and put him to flight, and he mimicked Raoul dodging around the tree-trunk. This angered Raoul, and when his orders to Outan to "shut up" passed unnoticed, he rushed at him and struck him in the face.

Now, although Outan looked upon both Madame de la Tour and Raoul as superior beings, and would have endured a great deal at their hands rather than displease them, still he had his own share of temper and pride, and this sudden blow from Raoul, given in the presence of his companions, filled him with fury. He struck back with all his might, and the next instant the two boys were rolling upon the ground in a mad grapple. At once they were surrounded by an eager circle of spectators, who keenly relished what promised to be a lively fight, and with excited cries urged on the youthful combatants.

So close were Raoul and Outan locked in each other's arms that they could not use their fists, and the struggle was therefore in reality not more than a wrestling-match.

But the more they strove the fiercer burned their rage, and the moment that one or the other did succeed in getting a hand free, cruel use would certainly be made of it.

While this was taking place Madame had been talking with some of the women, little imagining how Raoul was engaged, and she might have continued in her ignorance had not Outan's little sister run up to them, sobbing out something which her mother at once understood, and darted off with an exclamation of alarm.

This attracted Madame's attention, and more out of concern lest some accident should have happened than from curiosity, she followed the Indian woman. When they reached the crowd that surrounded the fighters, so densely packed was it that at first they could not get within sight of what was going on. But presently some of the men made space for Madame in rather a shamefaced way, until she was quite close to the struggling boys.

For a moment she thought it was only an innocent trial of strength, but a second look at their inflamed faces and furious eyes told her the truth, and in a horror-stricken voice she called out:

"Raoul! Raoul! what's the meaning of this? Stop it at once. I command you."

But Raoul was in too wild a fury to hear or heed, and, realizing this, Madame, the grace of whose form concealed an unusual degree of strength in a woman, laid hold of the boys and tore them apart.

CHAPTER IV

OFF TO THE WOODS

Raoul rose sullenly to his feet, and faced his aunt, who fixed upon him a look of stern displeasure mingled with sorrow.

"Oh, my nephew," she said in a tone of profound reproach, "are you not ashamed of yourself to be engaged in such an unseemly brawl? What an example to set those whom we are striving to teach better things! Come away, that I may have some talk with you in private."

Raoul, his anger now having in large part given place to shame, obeyed her bidding without a word, and they passed through the crowd into the forest. Here Raoul found his tongue, and explained how the thing had occurred. Madame heard him with attention and sympathy.

"You certainly had good reason to be provoked, my boy," she said as she tenderly patted his cheek. "But you must not forget that these poor people are heathens, and we are Christians, and that if we would win them over to be Christians also, we must do very differently from what they would do themselves. Now you must confess that you did not act in a Christian way, and I am very sorry. Let us pray to God to give us such self-control that we shall not fall into errors of this kind."

So they kneeled together upon the turf, and Raoul's heart was melted by the fervent prayer that came from his aunt's lips for the help of God in right living, and in the conversion of the Indians. Then, without delay, he sought out Outan, and, to the great surprise of the lad, expressed his regret for his hasty blow and begged his forgiveness.

To Outan the situation was so utterly novel that he was bewildered what to do, but obeying the impulse of his heart, he smiled broadly and gave Raoul a hearty hug, which showed in the clearest way that all ill-feeling had vanished from him.

The bear hunt having been successfully carried out, Madame and Raoul returned to Fort St. Louis, where they found Monsieur La Tour, who had got back from one of his trading expeditions, awaiting them in high spirits, because his business operations had been very successful.

Charles La Tour thought more of wealth and power than anything else in the world. Not even his beautiful, devoted wife was dearer to him. Yet he loved her after his own fashion, was very proud of her, and had not the slightest objection to her missionary zeal, so long as it did not cross any of his plans or ambitions. In regard to Raoul, of whom he was quite fond, he did think it rather a pity that he should be filled with his aunt's religious notions, because it might spoil him for the rough business of life; yet he made no protest against it, although he did now and then let drop a cynical speech that touched the boy's sensitive nature.

He had not been long at home before his restless spirit moved him to start off again, and this time he proposed that Raoul should accompany him.

"If your aunt can do without you for a few weeks, you'd better come with me," he said in his off-hand way, which took consent for granted. "You'll get some useful lessons in buying furs and trading goods, and in how to make good bargains with the Indians, if you keep your eyes and ears open."

Raoul, for his part, was quite eager to go. He loved adventure and excitement, and was very weary of the routine of life at the fort. So his response was no less hearty than prompt.

"Why, of course I want to go, uncle," he exclaimed, his face beaming with pleasure, and then checking himself as he thought of his aunt, he added in a more subdued tone, "If Aunt Constance is willing for me to go."

In her heart Madame would have very much preferred to have Raoul remain with her, but she was too unselfish to confess it, and smiled gaily enough as she said:

"Oh, I think I can manage to get along without you for a while, Raoul, although I shall of course miss you both greatly."

Winter was drawing near when the party set forth, and they must needs be not only well-armed, but well supplied with blankets and furs to resist the cold.

"THE PARTY SET FORTH."

There were twelve of them in all, six whites, and as many red men, stalwart fellows all of them, and thoroughly fitted to endure the hardships of their undertaking.

Madame was left in charge of the fort, with trusty old Simon Imbert as her lieutenant.

"My prayers will follow you every foot of the way, Charles," she said as she gave her husband a parting embrace, "and I shall be a happy woman when I see you safe back again."

La Tour's purpose was to go clear across the peninsula to the Bay of Fundy, seeking out the Indian encampments, buying whatever furs they had, and arranging for further supplies. He accordingly took with him a stock of goods such as pleased the Indian fancy.

Sufficient snow had already fallen to enable toboggans to be used, and with their baggage loaded upon these the party made good progress through the forest.

Raoul was in high spirits. Neither the toilsome tramping all day, nor the sleeping under the sky instead of in his own warm bed at night, nor the rude though abundant fare counted anything in comparison with his pride of filling a man's place, and, as far as was possible, doing a man's work.

There was one thing that gave him some trouble at first, however, until he solved the difficulty by being true to his best instincts.

His aunt had taught him to pray night and morning, and in the privacy of his own snug chamber in the fort he never omitted doing so; but when out in the forest in the company of men who took no thought for such things, it was very different.

Although his conscience pricked him sharply he let several days go by without prayers, just because he had not the courage to kneel down before the others.

But one night it seemed as if he could not get to sleep, he felt so conscience-stricken, and at last, unable to bear it any longer, he rolled out of his blankets, and kneeled against a tree-trunk.

A minute later his uncle, who had been out with some of his men setting traps, returned, and seeing Raoul, exclaimed in a tone of surprise:

"Hullo, my boy, what's the matter? Have you had a scare while I was away?"

Raoul, blushing deeply, rose to his feet, and with eyes fixed on the ground, murmured:

"No, sir, I was just saying my prayers, as I ought to have done every night, but I felt ashamed to."

It was on the tip of La Tour's tongue to say:

"Oh! leave that to your aunt. She can pray enough for both of us."

But he kept the words back, and with an indulgent smile which implied plainly that he thought the boy's occupation was of small consequence, he said in a kindly tone:

"Well, you'd better get back into your blankets again. We're going to have a stormy night, if I am not greatly mistaken."

That he had not mis-read the weather signs became evident ere midnight, for a snow-storm set in which grew in violence hour by hour, until by daylight it was so furious that not even Charles La Tour had the hardihood to brave it.

CHAPTER V

THE MOOSE HUNT

For several days the storm continued, and during that time no member of the party dared to leave camp, except to gather wood for the fire, which by great exertion and care was kept burning.

It was a miserable time for all. La Tour fumed and fretted at the delay, and the other whites shared his feelings, although the Indians seemed stolidly content with the forced inaction.

Temporary tents had been hastily made out of spruce boughs, and these being covered thickly with snow, afforded passable protection; yet they were poor places in which to spend a long day, and their occupants soon grew utterly weary of them.

Raoul was hard put to it to while away the dreary hours. His uncle was in too ill a humour to be pleasant company, and so the boy fell back upon the society of the men, who were inclined to be rough in their ways and coarse in speech.

On the evening of the third day of the storm La Tour called Raoul to him, and said in a sneering tone:

"How much good can your prayers do, think you? If you were to pray for the storm to stop, would it have any effect? You certainly couldn't wish a better chance to show what you can do."

Raoul was sorely puzzled to reply. He suspected that his uncle was only seeking to make fun of him, and yet it did not seem right to respond in the same spirit, thus making a jest of what was so sacred.

Looking very confused, he kept silence, until La Tour exclaimed impatiently:

"Have you lost your tongue? Why don't you answer me?"

"Because I don't know what to say," murmured Raoul. "Aunt Constance told me that we must not expect every prayer to be answered right away, and maybe even if she were to pray for the storm to stop it would not do it."

At this point La Tour's better nature asserted itself. He began to feel ashamed at thus teasing the boy, and to be impressed by his evident sincerity, so patting him affectionately upon the shoulder, he said:

"Don't mind my foolish words, Raoul. I didn't mean to hurt your feelings, or to weaken your faith. Keep on doing what you feel to be right, even if you are made fun of by those who ought to know better."

Raoul was deeply touched by these words, and thenceforward admired his uncle more than ever.

Ere he closed his eyes that night he did pray fervently for the storm to abate, and then curled up in his blankets to sleep as soundly as if in his own snug bed in Fort St. Louis.

He was awakened next morning by his uncle giving orders to the men in so cheery a tone that it was evident there had been a great change in his spirits; and, in making his way out of the half-buried tent, Raoul at once understood the reason, for the storm was all over, and the sun shone dazzlingly upon a world of spotless white.

"Good!" cried Raoul joyously. "Now we needn't stay here any longer. I am so glad," and he felt like dancing a little by way of expressing his feelings.

In his delight at the return of fine weather he might have forgotten to be thankful for the answer to his prayer, had not Monsieur La Tour reminded him by calling out:

"Good-morning, Raoul. You see the snow has ceased, and perhaps it was your prayers that caused it to stop."

Raoul laughed, and shook his head in disclaimer of such being the case.

"And now, uncle, we can be off again, can't we?" he responded. "I hope we won't have any more such storms."

In their journey across country they presently came to the region where huge moose, the grandest of all antlered animals, were to be found, and La Tour, as their supply of food was running low, decided to halt for a few days, in order that they might have a moose hunt.

This was good news to the whole party, and there was keen competition among the members to be allowed to take part in the hunt, La Tour's purpose being to have one-half of the men accompany him, while the rest remained at the camp.

Raoul took it for granted that he was to go, and was quite dismayed when his uncle let fall a remark which implied that he was to stay behind.

"Why, uncle," he exclaimed, "am I not to go with you?"

"Well, I hadn't thought about it, Raoul," was the reply. "Won't it be rather hard work for you to keep up with us? And then there may be some danger, you know."

"Oh, but I don't mind either the hard work or the danger," Raoul promptly responded. "Please let me go too, uncle, I want to so much."

"Very well then," replied La Tour, good-naturedly. "You can come along, but you'll have to look after yourself, for I'm going to give my whole attention to the moose."

Mounted upon broad snow-shoes, which enabled them to travel with ease and speed over the deepest snow, the hunting-party set forth amid the cheers of those who regretfully remained behind. They were all in high spirits, and the men made little boasts among themselves as to which of them would be the first to sight a moose, and to get the first shot at one.

"This heavy fall of snow will make things easier for us," Monsieur La Tour said to Raoul, as they tramped along together. "The big fellows will not be able to run very fast through such deep drifts."

It was not until mid-day drew near that signs of moose were seen, and then one of the keen-sighted Indians, who was in the van, came hurrying back to announce that he had found fresh tracks in the snow.

After examining them La Tour consulted for a moment with his companions, and then laid out his plan of campaign, which was that the party should spread out in a wide line, so as to cover as much ground as possible, and yet keep within hearing of signals, so as to be able to gather together again at the proper time.

"As for you, Raoul, you had better follow me," he said. "You'll not miss any of the excitement, and you'll be less likely to get astray."

This suited Raoul perfectly, and having seen to it that his gun was ready for instant action he followed his uncle's lead, although it was no easy matter to keep pace with his rapid stride.

On they went through the forest, with every sense alert to detect the proximity of their prey.

Presently La Tour stopped short, and bent his gaze intently to the right. Raoul looked in the same direction, but at first could not make out anything, yet from his uncle's action, it was plain that he must have sighted a moose, for he began to creep forward stealthily, with his gun held in readiness to fire.

Raoul, holding his breath, kept close behind, and at last his eyes fell upon a dark form scarcely distinguishable from the thick evergreen against which it stood.

"There he is! I see him!" he whispered to himself, while his heart throbbed wildly.

Just then La Tour levelled his gun, and the silence was shattered by its startling report.

A moment later the evergreens were violently agitated, and out of them rushed a huge bull moose, made furious by the wound, which at once charged fiercely down upon the hunters.

CHAPTER VI

IN THE NICK OF TIME

As it happened, the snow did not lie very heavily at this particular place, and the great creature was able to move with tremendous speed.

"Look out, Raoul!" shouted La Tour, as he darted aside to evade the moose's onset. "Get behind a tree, and then fire at him."

This was precisely what Raoul had in mind to do, and he made a gallant effort to accomplish it, but unfortunately in his haste he caught his snow-shoes together, and over he went headlong into the snow with such violence as to nearly bury himself.

Confused by the fall, and blinded by the snow, he lay there helplessly, while the bull moose, infuriated by its wound, and seeing only the prostrate boy to account for it, bore down upon him with murderous intent.

He fully realized his danger, and yet felt powerless to avert it, for to regain one's feet after a tumble with snow-shoes on is no easy matter.

In the meantime La Tour had rushed out from behind the tree, and by waving his arms and shouting, strove to attract the attention of the animal to himself until Raoul should have time to get upon his feet again, and find a place of safety.

But the moose was not to be thus diverted from its victim, and kept on until it was within ten yards of Raoul, whose fate now seemed to be sealed.

La Tour, quite forgetting himself in his anxiety for the boy, made a desperate effort to get in between him and the animal, and groaned aloud as he saw that it could not avail.

Then, suddenly, Raoul raised himself upon his knees, and pointing his gun at the moose's head, pulled the trigger.

"SUDDENLY, RAOUL RAISED HIMSELF UPON HIS KNEES."

At the report the big brute pitched forward upon its antlers, almost turning a somersault, and La Tour with an exclamation of joy ran to Raoul, and lifting him up clasped him to his breast, crying:

"Bravo! my nephew, bravo! That was a splendid shot. I never thought you could do it."

But hardly had the words left his lips than his exultation changed to alarm, for the moose, which had been only stunned by the bullet, and not mortally wounded, rose to its feet again to renew the charge.

Happily the shock of the bullet had bewildered it so that it went off at a tangent, and ere it could recover itself La Tour had hurried Raoul to safe shelter behind a mighty tree.

Hastily reloading his gun, an action which Raoul lost no time in imitating, La Tour watched his chance to give the great animal a final shot.

After plunging about for a little it once more located its assailants, and, looking very terrible in its rage, made another furious rush at them.

This they both evaded without difficulty, and then La Tour got the opportunity he sought, and sent a bullet into the heart of the mighty creature, which brought its career to a sudden end.

"Phew!" he exclaimed in a tone of profound relief, as he took off his fur cap and wiped the perspiration from his forehead. "That was lively work, wasn't it, Raoul? What a grand fight the old fellow did make! He pretty nearly had you under his hoofs. You managed to fire in the nick of time. That was a clever shot, my boy, and I am proud of you for it."

Raoul flushed with pleasure at his uncle's praise, which he appreciated all the more because La Tour was far more prone to find fault than to express approval.

"I thought it was all over with me, Uncle Charles," he said, "for the snow had got into my eyes so that I could not see properly, but I did the best I could."

"And a very good best it was, my boy. No man could have done better. You'll make a fine hunter when you're full grown. Ah, ha! here come some of the men. I wonder what fortune they have had."

Attracted by the sound of the firing, the rest of the hunting party had hurried to the scene, and La Tour was in his element as he proudly displayed the fallen monarch.

"Raoul and I are partners in him," he said laughingly. "Raoul hit him in the head, and I hit him in the heart, but he came within an ace of finishing Raoul first." And he then proceeded to relate what had happened.

Raoul was warmly congratulated upon his lucky escape, and upon the excellence of his marksmanship, and everybody rejoiced over the splendid prize which had been secured, for the moose was in superb condition, and would supply them with savoury steaks and roasts for many days.

After what had occurred at the moose hunt, it was evident that his uncle regarded Raoul in a different light. He dropped his bantering tone toward him, and treated him more on an equal footing, and Raoul fully appreciated the change.

During the remainder of their trip they were favoured with such good fortune—the game proving plentiful all along the route, and the Indians whose villages they visited being so well supplied with furs and so eager to trade—that La Tour, in high good humour, told Raoul he brought him good luck, and must accompany him again.

The whole party got back to Fort St. Louis without a mishap, and then everybody settled down for the winter, as there were to be no more trading expeditions.

But Madame La Tour did not suspend her missionary work because it was winter time. As soon as her husband had returned and relieved her of the charge of the fort, she resumed her visits to the Indian encampments. This was the best season for what she sought to accomplish, because the men were about the wigwams most of the time, and she could get a hearing from them as well as from the women and children.

Raoul usually went with her. He liked the idea of being in some sense her protector, and she was always such good company that the hours never seemed long that were spent in her society.

He always carried his gun, not that there was anything to fear from the Indians. They were altogether to be trusted. But some wild animal might be encountered that would venture to attack, or that might be worth having a shot at, any way.

Right glad he was that he did have his gun one afternoon when he and his aunt were returning from a day spent at the Souriquois village, where the good woman had been teaching the squaws, not only how to be Christians, but also how to be better wives and mothers.

They were walking rapidly, and talking busily, when a horrible scream that sent a chill of terror to their hearts, and caused them to stop suddenly in the path, issued from the thick woods in front of them.

A stranger would have been at a loss to guess what sort of creature could produce so frightful a sound, but Madame La Tour recognized it at once, and she perceptibly shrank closer to Raoul as she said in a startled voice:

"It is a *loup cervier*, Raoul, and right in our way!"

CHAPTER VII

AT CLOSE QUARTERS

Raoul knew the scream also, and something about the animal from whence it came, and he first looked carefully at his gun to make sure that it was ready for instant use, and then peered into the obscurity of the thick evergreens, in the attempt to locate the fierce brute which had thus challenged their passing.

What Madame meant by *loup cervier* was what is now known as the "Indian Devil," or catamount, a species of puma that could be very dangerous when in a fighting humour, as this one evidently was.

"Don't be frightened, Aunt Constance," said Raoul sturdily. "I'll shoot him dead the moment I see him," and he brought his gun to his shoulder as he spoke.

"Wait, wait until you can see him plainly," said Madame under her breath. "You must not miss."

There was a rustling among the branches, another blood-curdling scream, and then the hideous face of the creature appeared, its eyes flaming with fury, and its cruel teeth showing white among the rigid bristles that protruded from its furry cheeks.

Now if Raoul had been alone, he would assuredly have been nervous enough to make it a difficult matter to take good aim, but the presence of his aunt made him forget himself utterly in his loyal determination to protect her from the impending peril. He felt as firm as a rock. Not a nerve quivered, and, aiming straight between the baleful eyes, he fired.

The report rang out on the still evening air, and was instantly followed by a snarling shriek from the wounded animal, so charged with fury that Raoul instinctively pressed his aunt back out of the path.

30

Just as he did so the puma sprang at them, for it was not killed, a slight movement of its head as Raoul fired having caused the bullet to strike too high, and plough through the fur on the forehead, instead of burying itself in the brain.

Raoul's sudden movement caused the brute to fall short, and ere it could gather itself to spring again the boy, clubbing his gun, struck at it with the heavy butt.

It was the best thing to be done under the circumstances, and yet, when the maddened catamount, squirming around as if it were made of rubber, caught the stock in its teeth, and tore at the gun with its terrible claws, there seemed small chance of Raoul being able to repeat the blow.

Happily this was not necessary on his part, for Madame, who had been perfectly composed throughout, having picked up a stout stick, came to his assistance, and, with a clever blow delivered just behind the puma's ear, put an end to its existence.

"Bravo, Aunt Constance!" cried Raoul delightedly. "You've done for him, and just in time, too! He was pulling the gun out of my hands."

There was the light of triumph in Madame la Tour's fine eyes as she turned the dead thing over with her stick.

"He meant us mischief, Raoul," she said, "and he has paid dearly for it. If he had left us alone he would not be lying there now. Let us kneel down and thank God for our deliverance."

And so they knelt together, while Madame, in a few fervent sentences, expressed their gratitude to Providence for having thus protected them from injury.

As they hastened homeward, Madame said in a low tone, as if talking to herself rather than to Raoul:

"This is a wild, dangerous country, and I grow very weary of it. I pray that I may be spared to get back to France some day."

Raoul heard these words with some surprise. His aunt always seemed so busy and content in the doing of her duty, that he did not suppose she was not as happy as he was himself, but his quick sympathy inspired him to ask:

"Shall we be going back to France some day, Aunt Constance?"

"Only God knows that, my dear," was the reply. "I'm sure I cannot tell. We are in the hands of Providence, and whatever comes to pass will be the best."

Raoul said no more at the time, but thenceforward his admiration for his aunt was deepened by the knowledge that she would really prefer being across the ocean, although she always seemed so serene and satisfied with her lot in Acadia.

Monsieur La Tour was much interested in the account of the encounter with the catamount.

"You deserve credit, both of you," he said warmly. "As for you, my dear wife," he added, with an unusually loving look, "there seems to be no limit to your talents. You can preach, teach, hunt, fish, and look after the affairs of your own household better than any woman I ever knew. How fortunate I was to get such a wife! Eh, Raoul?"

Madame's noble countenance was flooded with colour by her husband's frank praise, which made her heart sing for joy, and going up to him, she threw her arms about his neck and kissed his bronzed cheek, saying:

"Thank you, my dear Charles, for your kind words, which I am sure are not empty ones."

With the return of spring, La Tour, whose enterprise and energy knew no bounds, unfolded a new plan he had formed for the extension of his power and the increase of his fortune.

This was the building of still another fort, and the site he had selected was the mouth of what is now the St. John River, in the province of New Brunswick, then known by the musical Indian name of Ouangondy.

This place had many advantages over Fort St. Louis. The river went far inland, and was the highway for many Indian tribes who had precious pelts to barter. Not only so, but the whole New England coast could be conveniently reached by canoe, or sailing shallop, and again, the lay of the land was such that an exceedingly strong position could be easily had.

Throughout the summer the building went on, and ere autumn came again the new fort, which La Tour modestly called after himself, was completed. It stood upon a rise of ground commanding the harbour and the sharp turn made by the river on entering, about half-a-mile below, the famous falls, which then as now worked both ways, pouring up river when the tide was high and down river when it was low.

Fort La Tour was solidly built of stone, and stood nearly two hundred feet square, with four bastions at the angles, and twenty good cannon frowning from the battlements. Without were sturdy palisades as a further protection, and within, two comfortable dwellings, a tiny chapel, and the necessary storehouses, barracks for the garrison, and other buildings.

Such was Raoul's new home, and he heartily approved of the change, because the country round about Fort La Tour was far richer and finer than that about Fort St. Louis, and the beautiful river held out promise of many a pleasant canoe trip, when the warm days of summer returned.

As for Madame La Tour, she felt sorry to leave her dusky charges when they seemed to promise such good results, but she consoled herself with the thought that there were plenty of others equally needing the light, and that she could continue her good work from the new fort.

CHAPTER VIII

A PERILOUS ENTERPRISE

Hitherto all had gone so well with Charles La Tour that he could hardly be blamed if he came to look upon himself as a favoured child of fortune. He had had the whole of Acadia to himself, so to speak, and what with fishing, fur-trading, and farming, had greatly increased his substance.

But now rumours of a rival came to disturb his peace. Another Charles, who was generally known as Charnace, had obtained from the French King certain grants and privileges in Acadia, and, wrath at finding La Tour already monopolizing the country, he let it be known that he proposed to contest the field with him by force of arms.

He chose his time well for the attack upon Fort La Tour, coming when the stock of provisions were lowest, the garrison smallest, and those whose support could be counted upon were most widely scattered, and he brought with him a strong force of soldiers in his four staunch vessels.

Stationing his two ships and the galiot so that they blockaded the ship channels, and the pinnace to the north-east of Partridge Island, he landed several hundred men so as to control the surrounding country, and then settled down for a siege, feeling quite confident that the capitulation of the fort was only a question of time.

In the meantime the commander of Fort La Tour had not been idle, although the coming of Charnace had been like a bolt out of the blue, for he did not expect to see anything of him that year. He lost no time in making preparations for a determined defence, in which his stout-hearted wife gave him efficient help. By means of spies, he got full information as to his enemy's purpose, and laughed grimly at the latter's threats.

"And so he has vowed that he will send me back to France in manacles, has he? Well, words are cheap. It is easy to indulge in big talk, but not always so easy to put it into deeds. We shall see how Monsieur Charnace will keep his word."

Raoul was not at all dismayed at being besieged. On the contrary, he was pleased by the prospect of exciting times, and promised himself to take as active a part in the defence as his uncle would permit.

"What right has Charnace coming here to attack us?" he asked with fine indignation at the insolence of the intruder. "We were here first, and he has no business interfering. We must give him such a beating that he will not dare to come near us again."

Keeping his ships well out of range of the cannon at the fort, and his men safely disposed in the protection of the woods, Charnace sought to cut off all supplies by sea or land, and thus let slow starvation win the day for him. Now La Tour was just then eagerly expecting the arrival from La Rochelle of the armed ship *Clement* with a full cargo of supplies of all sorts, and a goodly number of soldiers and colonists. In fact, the vessel was overdue, and if she should come up the bay without warning, she would assuredly be captured by Charnace's ships, which would have no difficulty in overpowering her.

"We must stop her before she comes too far," he said, "and yet I hardly know how it is to be managed. Charnace's spies and scouts are all around us. Have you any notion how it can be managed, Constance?" And, as was usually the case when in perplexity, he turned for counsel to the shrewd woman who was so peculiarly his helpmate.

"Let us send for Joe Takouchen," was her reply. "He may think of a way."

Accordingly Joe was sent for, and promptly appeared, his usually impassive countenance betraying curiosity as to the reason for the summons.

Joe was a splendid specimen of the Souriquois, who worshipped Madame La Tour as though she were divine. She had been particularly kind both to himself and his family, and he was ready to risk his life for her on any occasion. The situation was explained to Joe, while he listened in silence, but with a comprehending expression. Then, nodding his head sagely, he said:

"Joe will take the message to the ship. He will go to-night."

"And how will you manage it, Joe?" asked La Tour.

Joe smiled significantly, and explained that his plan was to steal out of the fort at night, make his way to the headlands south-west, and thence put off in a canoe, as soon as the supply ship came in sight. La Tour's face lit up at the proposition.

"It's a big risk, Joe, but if any man alive can carry the thing out it is you. Whom will you take with you?"

Joe replied that Jean Pitchebat, a stalwart Frenchman, who was his special friend, would be his choice, and La Tour approved.

Raoul, who had been a silent listener hitherto, now spoke up.

"May I go with Joe too, Uncle Charles?" he asked, in a tone whose anxiety showed how fully he was in earnest.

La Tour looked at the boy with such manifest surprise that the latter flushed hotly. Yet, being full of his desire, he turned to Joe and said entreatingly:

"You will not mind taking me, will you?"

Joe glanced inquiringly at his master and mistress. He was very fond of Raoul, and had no objection to taking him along, but he felt that the matter was not one for him to settle. La Tour had it on the tip of his tongue to brusquely refuse Raoul's request, but the expression on his wife's face made him pause, and before he spoke, she said in her gentle way:

"You might let him go, Charles. He will be in God's hands. There is danger everywhere now, and his heart is set upon going."

"Oh, very well, then, so long as Joe is willing. What do you say, Joe?" and La Tour turned to the taciturn Indian.

"Joe say all right," was the laconic response, at which Raoul clapped his hands gleefully.

They set off the same night. Fortunately it was both dark and windy, so that there was all the less danger of their movements being seen or heard. But they must needs exercise the utmost caution, for Charnace had many Indians in his service, and they would no doubt be acting as scouts and sentinels in the neighbourhood of the fort.

Joe led the way with amazing dexterity, stepping over the ground as silently as a serpent, and the other two followed, doing their best to imitate him. Several times he stopped short, peered eagerly into the darkness, listened intently for a moment, and then, muttering something which Raoul could not catch, changed his course to right or left.

"JOE LED THE WAY."

Once the sound of voices came out of the night to them, and Raoul's heart throbbed wildly. He was not so much afraid of being captured as he was that they should be balked in their purpose, and that the supply ship, coming up without warning, would fall into Charnace's hands. They were evidently passing through the line of their enemy's sentinels, and in peril of being betrayed by the slightest sound. Very cautiously did Joe make his way, now turning this way and now that, while Raoul and Jean kept so close that they could almost touch him.

It was trying work, that told upon muscles and nerve, yet Raoul held his own with the men all right, and certainly moved as silently as Jean, even if he could not quite equal Joe.

At last they seemed to be getting well away from the fort, and into safer ground, when suddenly a dark form rose in front of them.

CHAPTER IX

THE STOPPING OF THE SUPPLY SHIP

Joe crouched low, preparing for a spring. Jean and Raoul did likewise, and not one of them breathed.

"Who goes there?" demanded a rough, stern voice, but the next instant it was silenced, for Joe, throwing himself upon the speaker with a leap like that of a panther, brought him to the ground with his hands at his throat.

But the man lay so motionless in his grip that there was no need to take his life. In falling backward, his head had struck a stone, and he was senseless. As soon as Joe realized this he let go of him, and whispering to his companions:

"Quick—quick—run!" he darted off with them at his heels.

Not trying to pick their steps, they plunged through the darkness as fast as they could, slipping, stumbling, tripping, yet keeping on desperately, for they knew not if the whole camp might not presently be upon their heels.

There was a stir among Charnace's sentinels and a calling to one another, but none of them knew in which direction the fugitives had gone, and after some aimless scurrying about they gave up all idea of pursuit, and settled down to quiet again.

Meanwhile, the three had continued their wild flight until their breath was spent, and then they threw themselves down to recover it.

"All right now," said Joe, nodding complacently. "We see no more of them," and he was quite correct. They were now beyond Charnace's lines, and could pursue their way in a more leisurely fashion. The break of day found them far down the shore and drawing near an encampment of friendly Indians. From these Joe had no difficulty in obtaining a good canoe, and a supply of provisions, and by noon they were out on the Bay of Fundy, watching for the *Clement*.

The weather was fine, and Raoul keenly enjoyed dancing over the white-capped waves in their buoyant craft, which Joe and Jean managed with such matchless skill. They did not expect him to paddle, and so he stretched himself out in the bottom of the canoe and took his ease, the excitement and exertion of the past night having pretty thoroughly tired him.

For some hours no sign of the ship appeared, and then, as the afternoon drew towards its close, Joe's keen eyes descried a sail showing above the horizon to the southward.

"Good!" he grunted, and with a sweep of his paddle he turned the canoe in that direction.

"You paddle now," he said to Raoul, and the latter obeyed. Propelled by the three blades, into which the paddlers put their strength, the light craft bounded over the water towards the ship.

"Oh! I hope it is the *Clement*" said Raoul. "We shall be just in good time."

Mile after mile they swept along, until Raoul's arms began to ache, and his breath to become scant, but Joe and Jean were pegging away as vigorously as at first, and he hated to give up. They were nearing the ship rapidly, and ere long would be close enough to hail her, when, to their surprise, she came about, and went off on another tack, leaving them rapidly astern.

"Hullo!" exclaimed Raoul in a tone of consternation. "What did she do that for? We shall soon be farther away from her than we were at first."

Joe stopped paddling for a moment, and looked very cross. Then, rising to his full height, he swung the paddle above his head, hoping to attract the attention of some one on board the vessel. But it had no effect. The ship continued in her course, and, there being plenty of wind, her speed was so great as to make it useless for the canoe to follow her.

"RISING TO HIS FULL HEIGHT, JOE SWUNG THE PADDLE ABOVE HIS HEAD."

The occupants of the canoe looked blankly at each other. Even the usually impassive Joe did not disguise his chagrin, while Jean sought relief for his feelings in some strong language that would have brought upon him a reproof from Madame La Tour had she been present. The sun had already set. Night was drawing near, and unless they reached the ship before darkness fell they might miss her altogether, and she would go on to become a prize for the waiting Charnace. Raoul clearly realized their critical position, and while Joe and Jean discussed what should be done, he lifted up his heart in earnest prayer that God would guide them to the ship even through the darkness.

Rested by their brief halt, the paddlers resumed work, steering the canoe straight up the Bay, so as if possible to intercept the vessel in her next tack. Meanwhile the daylight faded out of the sky, the wind dropped, and the water became perfectly calm. In almost complete silence the canoe glided steadily forward, Raoul, who had paddled until he was tired, once more taking it easy in the bottom.

Suddenly there came through the gloom the sound of a man's voice giving a command, and it made the hearts of those in the canoe leap for joy. Joe and Jean had been paddling listlessly, but now they went to work with fresh energy. Their light craft shot over the smooth water in the direction of the voice, and, a few minutes later, the dark bulk of the ship they sought loomed up before them.

Jean promptly hailed her, and was bidden to come alongside. A rope was thrown, whereby all three clambered up, and the next instant stood on the deck of the *Clement*. Very hearty was their welcome here.

The Captain of the good ship felt deeply grateful for the timely warning, and offered his wearied and hungry visitors the best at his disposal, while the colonists and others crowded about, eager to be told about La Tour and his forts, and how things were going in the new world to which they had come. Raoul was pleased to find himself a person of some importance, and his tongue wagged merrily as he answered the many questions poured upon him, or in his turn made inquiries on his own account. Ere he lay down that night in the Captain's cabin, he did not forget to thank God for having answered his prayer by guiding the canoe into the way of the *Clement*.

After consulting with Joe and Jean, the Captain of the *Clement* decided that the best plan would be for him to keep the ship off for the present, as it was not likely Charnace would break his blockade of Fort La Tour to go after her, and, even if he did, she could easily over-match any one of his vessels, and sail away from any of them.

In the meantime, Joe and Jean would make their way back to the fort, leaving Raoul on board. This arrangement was carried out successfully. The messengers again passed through Charnace's lines and brought their good news to La Tour, who at once decided that the best thing to be done was for him to get on board the *Clement* and sail on her for Boston, to obtain reinforcements against the enemy. So, on a dark, still night a canoe, containing both Monsieur and Madame, glided unseen past the blockading vessels, La Tour smiling grimly, and Constance giving a shudder as they heard Charnace's own voice saying:

"The spy who just came from the fort says that his comrades will send down La Tour in shackles at midnight," little knowing that the rascally conspirators had been discovered, and were themselves now lying in irons in the dungeon of the fort.

<h1 style="text-align:center">CHAPTER X</h1>

<h2 style="text-align:center">ADVENTURE IN BOSTON</h2>

The *Clement* was found and boarded without much difficulty, and at daybreak she was on her way to Boston, bearing the La Tours and Raoul.

They were well received at the quaint capital of the New England Province, and, after a good deal of negotiation, for the shrewd colonists knew how to drive good bargains, La Tour succeeded in arranging for four ships, carrying nearly two score guns, and one hundred and fifty men. With this force he felt quite equal to getting the better of his rival, and set sail from Boston in high spirits. For six weeks Fort La Tour had been silent as a tomb, the besiegers, who were quite unaware of the La Tours having slipped away, trusting to starvation to do their work for them, while the garrison, looking forward to their commander's return in force, made no attempt at sorties, but got along, as best they could, on the scanty rations left them. They kept a sharp and steady look-out, however, and one day their eyes were gladdened by the sight of many sails in the offing.

"La Tour! La Tour!" they cried joyously, and at once proceeded to welcome him with a salute in which every cannon on the ramparts had a part. La Tour did his best to capture some of Charnace's vessels, but both wind and tide favoured their escape, although he chased them as far as the Penobscot. There was great rejoicing at the fort, and feasting followed famine for the remainder of the week.

"Will Monsieur Charnace come back again, do you think?" Raoul asked of his aunt as they sat in her room, having grown weary of the revelling.

"I am afraid so," she answered with a sigh. "He is a proud, determined man, and this defeat will only cause him to try again with a stronger force. I fear there is trouble in store for us."

44

"But why can't he leave us alone?" Raoul cried petulantly. "We have never made any attack upon him."

"Because this world, big as it may seem, Raoul, is all too small for such men as your uncle and Charnace," Madame replied. "They cannot brook a rival, and they must needs fight until one or the other is overthrown," and she sighed again deeply, for her gentle heart shrank from conflict, and she infinitely preferred teaching religion to the Indians, to all her husband's grand plans for wealth and power.

Foiled in his first attempt, but not shaken in his purpose, Charnace went off across the ocean to France to see if something could not be done there to humble his rival, and La Tour was left to pursue his way in peace.

Raoul now took an active part in what went on, and led quite a busy life. He accompanied his uncle in his trips up the River St. John, where they met with Indians from the interior, who brought rich furs to barter for goods. Twice he crossed over to Fort St. Louis, and each time congratulated himself on the move to Fort La Tour; and what pleased him most of all, he was allowed to go on one of the ships to Boston, for he had very pleasant recollections of his first visit there. His visit was made memorable by an experience which was certainly of too exciting a nature to be soon forgotten. Having a leisure afternoon, he went off alone for a stroll along the river-bank, where he felt sure he would find something to interest him. And in this he was not disappointed.

He had gone about half-a-mile from the town when, seeing a group of boys evidently much interested in something, he hurried towards them. To his surprise he saw that they were making sport of a strange-looking lad of about his own age, who seemed to be only half-witted. They wanted him to go into the water, but he held back in a terror-stricken way that ought to have caused them to desist, but only served to spur them on. Just as Raoul reached them, they had dragged the poor fellow to the edge of a little point below which the water was fairly deep, and, crying out: "Give him a dip; he needs a good wash!" were about to shove him over the edge, when Raoul, stirred to such indignation that he quite forgot that he stood alone against half-a-dozen, called out:

"Shame! Shame! Let the poor fellow be! Why do you torment him so?" and springing into their midst, he tore them away from their victim, and set him free.

So sudden was his onset—for the boys, being intent upon their *fun*, had not noticed his approach—that they were completely taken aback, and the idiot boy, finding himself free, had sufficient sense to make a break, whereby he got out of their reach ere they recovered from their surprise. Then they turned upon Raoul, and with coarse oaths demanded who he was, and what business he had interfering with them. Raoul realized that he was in a pretty tight place, and had no idea just how he was to get out of it, but he put on a bold front and replied:

"It's no matter who I am. You had no right to be tormenting that poor chap."

"Oh, ho! he's a Frenchie. Let us put him in instead," was the cry raised, and at once they threw themselves upon Raoul.

There were none of them larger than he, but they were six to one, and, although he fought splendidly, they were not long in bringing him to the ground. Seizing him roughly by the arms and legs they bore him to the edge of the bank, and in another instant they would have pitched him over, when a commanding voice shouted:

"Stop! Let that boy alone!" and again the young rowdies were checked in their rough sport. This time the interposition came from no less important a personage than Governor Winthrop himself, who, chancing to take his afternoon constitutional in that direction, had observed the disturbance, and hurried up to ascertain its meaning. He carried a stout cane, and followed up his command by laying it upon the backs of the boys nearest him with such good effect that they dashed off howling, and in a moment Raoul was left free to pick himself up and arrange his disordered dress.

"Pray, sir, what were they doing to you?" inquired Governor Winthrop with grave concern.

"They were trying to throw me into the river," responded Raoul, "and but for you, sir, they would have done it." And then he went on to explain what had taken place, while the Governor listened with an approving smile; and when he had finished, he placed his hand upon Raoul's shoulder, saying:

"You have borne yourself nobly, my son, and I feel ashamed that the children of our own townspeople should behave in so unseemly a fashion. And now tell me who are you and whence you come, for you are assuredly a stranger here."

When he learned that Raoul was the nephew of Charles La Tour, Lieutenant-General of Acadia, his interest manifestly deepened.

"Indeed, indeed," he said. "I know your worthy uncle well, and hold him in high esteem. You must come and sup with me, and I shall see that you return to your ship in due time."

Raoul was only too glad to accept such an attractive invitation, and so the close of this eventful day found him the guest of the Governor, and keenly relishing the excellent fare that his table afforded.

CHAPTER XI

TRAITORS IN THE CAMP

Madame La Tour greatly enjoyed Raoul's relation of his Boston experience.

"You see, virtue is not always merely its own reward," she said, smiling proudly upon her nephew. "It is sometimes well rewarded in other ways. Be ever ready to champion the weak and the innocent, Raoul. They are God's children, and you are doing His work when you take their part against the wicked and cruel people, of which, alas! there seems to be too many in this world."

The summer passed into autumn, and the autumn into winter, without bringing anything of special moment into the lives of those at Fort La Tour, save somewhat disquieting rumours of the intentions of Charnace.

It was said that he had gone to France to obtain the revocation of La Tour's commission as Lieutenant-General of Acadia, and authority to take him prisoner, and send him back to be imprisoned in the Bastile.

Now Charnace was known to have great influence at Court, and in those days, when the French kings so lightly valued their possessions in America, and did pretty much what those who had most influence over them advised, there was no telling how far Charnace might succeed in his hostile plans.

Accordingly La Tour set himself to prepare for the danger then threatening him, while his good wife prayed that, in some way, further conflict might be averted.

With the coming of spring, the news was confirmed by the appearance of Charnace in the ship *St. Francis* and his sending a messenger to demand La Tour's surrender.

To this La Tour defiantly replied that he would not give up either himself or his fort, so long as he had a pound of powder left; and Charnace, not being ready for an attack just then, withdrew to the Penobscot, where he had a fort of his own, to prepare for another siege.

Great was the concern now at Fort La Tour, whose commander bestirred himself in every way to meet the crisis. Unfortunately, circumstances were not in his favour. His trading had not prospered of late, and he had been compelled to mortgage his fort and all his real and personal property to a merchant in Boston as security for a large loan, in order to meet the demands upon him, and now he required a larger supply of ammunition, and, if possible, some more men. In this emergency he decided to make a flying trip to Boston in quest of both, trusting to get back ere Charnace reappeared.

Ere he left he called his wife, Raoul, Joe Takouchen, and Jean Pitchebat to him, and explained his purpose.

"I know it's a risk," he said, "but there seems no help for it. Without powder we cannot hold the fort, but with a good supply of it we can beat off this villain Charnace. Constance, I leave you in command. You, Raoul, will be her lieutenant, and you, Joe and Jean, her right-hand men. I know that I can trust you all to the uttermost." And, having thus spoken, he was about to dismiss them, when Madame, whose beautiful countenance had of late worn an anxious expression, for she fully realized the danger, said softly—

"Charles, let us kneel down and ask for God's protection from the enemy, for without His blessing your best plans will be of no avail."

So they all knelt, while Madame prayed with profound fervour for divine help, and, when they rose, her face had regained its wonted serenity.

Raoul felt quite flattered at being joined with his aunt in the charge of the fort. It seemed, in some sort, a recognition of his being more than a boy, and he vowed in his heart that he would show himself worthy of the confidence reposed in him.

Followed by his wife's prayers, and the anxious thoughts of the garrison, La Tour set sail for Boston.

He had not been gone long before a startling discovery was made by Raoul. Although the majority of those connected with the fort were Huguenots, the remainder were Catholics, and for their benefit La Tour tolerated the presence of two Jesuit priests named Miraband and Oriani.

Towards these men Raoul held feelings of cordial dislike. They had done their best to change his faith, using in vain the sly and subtle methods for which their Order has ever been notorious, but, instead of winning him over they had only aroused his antagonism.

Now it chanced that Raoul had been out shooting in the afternoon, and was returning to the fort, when, being weary, he sat down in a snug nook near the Falls to rest, and, before he knew it, was asleep.

Presently he was awakened by the sound of voices engaged in earnest talk, and, peeping through the thick foliage which hid him completely, he saw Miraband and Oriani.

Suspecting that this secret meeting meant some mischief, he felt no scruples about playing the part of listener.

The first few words confirmed his suspicions, and as they went on, his heart grew hot with indignation and wrath, for it became clear to him that these men, who had been so well treated at Fort La Tour, were in reality Charnace's spies, and had been keeping him informed of all that took place.

"The villains!" muttered Raoul under his breath. "They deserve to be hung, even if they are priests. I must let Aunt Constance know at once."

He did not stir until the two wicked plotters had finished their conference and gone off, and then he made all haste to the fort.

Madame La Tour was not entirely taken by surprise at his information. She herself had mistrusted these Jesuits, and had even warned her husband against them, but he had laughed the matter off, saying she was mistaken.

Now, she sent for her trusty Joe and Jean, to whom Raoul re-told his story.

They were mightily enraged at this treachery, and cried out for the hanging of the spies in the gate of the castle; and had La Tour himself been present, this would undoubtedly have been done, despite their sacred calling, which they had so dishonoured.

But Madame was too tender of heart to take such extreme measures. Good reason as she had to hate the whole Jesuit body, apart from the villainy of these two members of it, she shrank from following the advice of her counsellors, and to their frankly-expressed disgust did no more than to summon Miraband and Oriani before her, upbraid them with their treachery, adding some bitter words as to their being wolves in sheep's clothing, and then ordered them to be set adrift in a light canoe.

"Betake yourselves to your employer," she said with withering scorn, presenting a splendid picture of righteous indignation, as she towered above the cowering priests. "He is fit company for you. You have no right amongst honest men."

Raoul saw them into the canoe. He heartily agreed with Joe and Jean that the punishment was altogether inadequate, but he was too loyal to his aunt not to carry out her bidding; and as the Jesuits, who had wisely kept silence through it all, paddled off, he called after them:

"You've got off with your lives this time. But if my uncle ever catches you, it will be different."

CHAPTER XII

A GLORIOUS VICTORY

It was not a wise, even if it were a womanly, step on Madame La Tour's part to let the Jesuits go, for they, of course, made their way directly to Charnace, and acquainted him with the true state of affairs at the fort—La Tour absent in quest of reinforcements, only fifty men in the garrison, and the supply of powder and shot unduly low.

"Ah, ha!" chuckled Charnace, rubbing his hands. "You bring good news. My time has come. I would prefer not having to fight with a woman, but since La Tour has seen fit to desert his post, he must take the consequences."

Meantime, Madame La Tour, with her faithful supporters, strained every effort to prepare for the assault that could not be long delayed. Everything that could be secured in the way of food was packed into her storehouses; the scanty stock of ammunition was carefully examined and apportioned, so as to be used to the best advantage, and the little garrison was divided up into four watches, of which Madame took command of one, while Raoul, Joe and Jean captained the others, and then, as Madame said:

"We have done all that we can. We now leave ourselves in the hands of God."

Many days of suspense followed, and then the report came from a watcher on the headland, that three large ships were approaching.

Raoul received it first, and hastened to his aunt.

"It is Charnace," she said. "The crisis has come. God grant us strength and wisdom according; to our need."

Confident of an easy victory, Charnace sailed right up within cannon-range, and, having anchored, sent one of his captains ashore under a flag of truce to demand the surrender of the fort, coupling the demand with the threat that, if not immediately complied with, he would level the fort to the ground.

Raoul intently watched his aunt's face as she listened to the message. He devoutly hoped she would not surrender, but he knew better than to volunteer his opinion.

"Be good enough to say to Monsieur Charnace from me that until he has laid the walls of Fort La Tour level with the ground, it shall not be surrendered."

"I cannot but admire your courage, Madame, although I beg to doubt the wisdom of your decision," responded the captain, bowing low, while Raoul gave a cheer in which the others joined.

The instant the captain returned to the ship the flag of truce was lowered, and with the crash and roar of the first broadside the battle began.

Now among Madame La Tour's many accomplishments, was skill in the firing of big guns. This she had acquired when a mere girl at La Rochelle, and she had kept her hand and eye in by occasional practice after coming to Acadia.

It was therefore but natural that she should direct the firing from the fort, and so, posting herself in one of the bastions, with Raoul as her *aide-de-camp* to fly to and fro with orders, she pointed the first cannon with her own hands.

BEFRIENDED BY BRUIN

One of the noble families of Lorraine has a curious crest. It represents a big black bear in an iron cage, and recalls the legend as to the founding of the fortunes of the house, which runs somewhat in this way.

Several centuries ago there lived in the city of Nancy a little Savoyard named Michel, whose lot was certainly about as hard as a ten-year-old boy could endure without giving up life altogether. He was a homeless orphan, dependent entirely upon the alms of the charitable, for which he begged through the stony streets. A more pitiable appearance than he presented could scarcely be imagined. Privation and hunger had blanched his cheeks and shrunken his form. With his haggard face, half hidden by long disordered locks of a slightly reddish tinge, his bones showing through the thin ragged garments from which the sun and rain had taken all colour, he wearily dragged himself barefoot from door to door, meeting with many a harsh repulse, and but few kindly responses to his appeals.

His eyes alone showed any sign of spirit. They were of a deep blue tint, and in spite of his sufferings, held a strange sparkle that sometimes startled those who caught it.

At night, in company with some other street arabs of his own age, he found shelter in a wretched cellar kept by a villainous old hag, who made her lodgers pay nearly all they had, with such difficulty, begged during the day, for the privilege of sleeping upon mouldy straw pallets. The miserable place was draughty, damp and pestilential, but it was the only lodging the poor boys could afford, and offered at least some protection from the merciless cold of winter.

In that cellar there would only too often be heard through the hours of darkness heart-breaking sobs that refused to be suppressed, or the piteous moan, "I am so hungry, oh, I am so hungry!"

And sometimes in the morning, when the old hag would seek to clear her cellar of its occupants, screaming at them and striking them with her broom, there would be one who paid no heed to either screams or blows, but remained motionless on his pallet, for he had passed into the sleep that knows no waking.

Each day Michel grew paler, thinner, feebler, a cruel cough racking his slender frame as he shivered in his rags and tatters. Every limb ached, and sometimes it seemed to him as if he must lie down on the snow to die.

Late one afternoon, crouched in the corner of the doorway of the Duke's palace, and waiting for some one to pass by of whom he might beg alms, he wept bitterly. He was starving and freezing, but nothing came his way; yet to return to the cellar he did not dare. The old hag had a flinty heart which nothing save money could soften, and he was without a sou.

Overcome with despair at his condition, and horror at the thought of spending the night in the street, he fell on his knees and, lifting his tear-filled eyes to the darkening sky, put forth this pathetic prayer:

"O God in Heaven, take me to my mother!"

Just then a deep growl came from somewhere behind him and interrupted his prayer. He sprang up and looked about him.

The street was silent and deserted. The snow fell softly. A grating near the ground attracted his attention, and without stopping to consider, he said to himself that possibly if he passed through it he might find a good place to sleep.

He was exceedingly thin, and the bars of the grating widely placed, so that he had no difficulty in squeezing through. But imagine his consternation on finding himself face to face with an enormous black bear, into whose cage he had thus ventured to intrude.

"Oh, oh, what's the meaning of this!" demanded the astonished bruin in his own language.

He had just disposed of a good supper, and was feeling in particularly good trim, when poor Michel so unexpectedly tumbled into his presence. Angered at being disturbed, he made ready to demolish the impertinent intruder with his mighty paw. The little Savoyard, pale and tearful, kept perfectly still while he continued his prayer:

"O God in Heaven, take me to my mother, who went to you to beg for bread for her boy——"

A hot breath played upon his cheek.

"O Lord..." he moaned.

He thought he was as good as dead, and yet it seemed to him that something licked his face gently.

When, a few moments later, he realized that he was not being devoured—that he was still unharmed—he opened his eyes wide and they encountered those of the bear full of kindness and good humour.

This gave him courage. He got up. He patted the black muzzle of the big creature, which received the caress with a murmur of pleasure.

The stress of the day had so exhausted Michel that the moment his terror left him, he, with surprising unconcern, threw himself down to sleep.

The bear, as if flattered by the confidence thus shown in him, regarded him in a friendly fashion, then lay down beside him, almost completely enveloping him with his warm fur, and so fell asleep in his turn.

Now this bear was no other than the famous "Mascot," who was maintained at the palace as a representative of the Canton of Berne, in recognition of the valuable services rendered by the Swiss to the people of Lorraine in their struggle with the Duke of Burgogne.

Mascot was an important figure at the Court of Duke Leopold. Everything possible was done for his comfort. He had his own attendant, whose sole duty was to care for his person and to minister to his every want. In his spacious cage he could move about freely and swing at ease his heavy head.

Every afternoon he was visited by the courtiers, and sometimes even by the Duke; but he troubled himself very little concerning the one or the other. Indifferent to everything, even the ducal smile, he gazed stolidly upon the folk, who did not interest him in the least. His superb fur was greatly admired, but not his unsociable disposition. And so he passed the days, promenading up and down his cage, swinging his head to and fro for hours at a time, eating, drinking, and sleeping in seemingly perfect content, and regarded with profound respect by his numerous visitors.

On the morning after Michel made his way into the cage he awoke at daybreak. Bewildered at his strange situation, yet delighted because of the comfortable night he had passed snuggled up in the bear's thick warm fur, he made haste to get out in the same manner that he had entered, not forgetting, however, to give his kind host a hearty hug expressive of his gratitude. He had no idea of losing so excellent a sleeping-place by remaining in it too long and being discovered by the bear's attendant. That day fortune favoured him in his begging, and he was able to obtain the food he so sadly needed. As it was still very cold he impatiently awaited the return of night in order to regain his snug refuge.

On re-entering the cage the bear gave him a kinder welcome than the first time, and henceforward the two were great friends. Every morning the little Savoyard slipped away unseen, and every night returned to his shaggy benefactor. Thanks to the comfort he then enjoyed, his appearance began to improve. His shrunken limbs rounded out again and the colour came back to his cheeks. But this could not go on indefinitely. One fine day the bear's attendant was filled with astonishment at finding a small boy sleeping beside Mascot, who was licking him softly. He thought he must have lost his senses, when he beheld the little fellow wake up and caress the fierce brute in his turn without showing the slightest sign of fear.

His outcries attracted the attention of a groom, and he told the strange news to a footman, who passed it on to the pages, and they spread it about the palace so thoroughly that presently everybody, including Duke Leopold himself, was hurrying towards the cage.

There they found poor Michel, weeping piteously and evidently in terror of being harshly dealt with. Having soothed him with a few kind words, the Duke ordered him he could, told his story. Touched by the recital of his sufferings, and animated by a worthy determination not to be outdone in generosity by a bear, the Duke offered Michel a place in his household.

to come out of the cage and explain himself. The boy promptly obeyed, and, as best

The little Savoyard did not hesitate to accept, and presently found himself in what seemed like paradise, after the miseries he had been enduring.

Clothed in fine raiment and faring sumptuously every day, he soon developed into a handsome lad. His spirit grew with his body. He took an ardent interest in the sports and martial exercises of his companions, and in due time he became the most expert of them all in the use of bow and sword and lance.

Withal, remaining modest in manner, respectful to his superiors, and devoted to the Duke, he rapidly rose in the latter's service through the grades of squire, knight and count, until he came to be the second person in the realm, and the founder of a family enjoying large possessions and great influence.

Nor was he ungrateful to the animal which had befriended him in his extremity. So long as Mascot lived he visited him constantly. Their friendship never cooled, and when the one-time beggar was entitled to choose a crest for himself, he gave orders that it should be a big black bear in an iron cage.